SUMMER
NITES

SUMMER NITES

JEREMEY NOLLETT

Summer Nites

Copyright © 2020 by Jeremey Nollett. All rights reserved.

No part of this publication may be reproduced, stored in a retrieval system or transmitted in any way by any means, electronic, mechanical, photocopy, recording or otherwise without the prior permission of the author except as provided by USA copyright law.

This novel is a work of fiction. Names, descriptions, entities, and incidents included in the story are products of the author's imagination. Any resemblance to actual persons, events, and entities is entirely coincidental.

The opinions expressed by the author are not necessarily those of URLink Print and Media.

1603 Capitol Ave., Suite 310 Cheyenne, Wyoming USA 82001
1-888-980-6523 | admin@urlinkpublishing.com

URLink Print and Media is committed to excellence in the publishing industry.

Book design copyright © 2020 by URLink Print and Media. All rights reserved.

Published in the United States of America

ISBN 978-1-64753-301-4 (Paperback)
ISBN 978-1-64753-302-1 (Digital)

30.03.20

1

It was a nice summer evening, and I decided to go for a walk. The warm, gentle breeze slightly blowing my hair. Off in the distance, you can see the rain clouds moving in from the west. In the distance, lighting lights up the sky and claps of thunder rumble in the air. You could hear the laughter and whispers of people in the background.

As I walk, I hear footsteps in the distance behind me. I pay no attention to them as I'm lost in my own thoughts, but I still know there is a presence behind me. So I picked up my pace. As I do, so do the footsteps behind me. I stop, so do they. I slowly turn to see who is behind me. By now the wind is picking up and the rain is coming. Lightning lights up the sky as the storm grows closer. Thunder rumbles louder and louder. My heart is pounding. I slowly turn. As I get to where I can see through the corner of my eye nothing is there.

So I continue on at a faster clip. Then I hear the footsteps again, only faster now. I'm too scared to stop to see what or who is behind me. I began to jog, trembling in fear. My heart feels like it's going to jump out of my chest. I'm searching like a wild animal for an escape. The footsteps are now getting louder and faster. I want to scream out for help but can't. The rain is now pouring down. The wind is blowing stronger and stronger by the minute. The street seems to never end.

I begin to run at a full sprint now, but so do the footsteps behind me. My mind says, "Run, you fool," but I stop. The footsteps don't! I'm stuck, frozen in my tracks. Then I decided to turn to see what or who was coming behind me. Suddenly it was like I was hit by a Mack truck. Pain like I've never felt in my life. I feel something running down my back. I thought maybe it's the rain. I reach around too feel what it was. As I bring my hand around, I see it's blood.

I try to run for help but drop to my knees, then to my belly lying face down in a puddle of water. A towering man stands in front of me. As I fade out of consciousness, all I can make out is a dirty smirk on his face. I can't get a detailed picture of his attributes, just that smirk as I fade in and out. I wonder to myself what I did to deserve this. I hear yelling a distance behind me and then footsteps, again trying not to pass out.

I try to move in case it was him again. There is a little place to hide around the corner behind the big blue trash bin. If I can just get to it. The footsteps are getting closer. I try pulling myself down the sidewalk then I feel someone grabbed me.

I cringe in fear while also trying to stay awake long enough to survive. Then I hear, "You're gonna be okay, help is on the way!"

When I awoke in the hospital, nurses and a tall, funny-looking man in blue scrubs was standing around my bed.

"Where am I?" I asked.

"You're in the hospital. Do you know what happened?" the doctor answered.

"No, I don't. I just remember being chased, then severe pain in my back area."

"Do you know who did this?"

"No!"

"Well, you are very lucky to be alive. You were stabbed just below the heart!"

As the doctor and nurses walked away, I take a sigh of relief. Moments later, I hear the doctor talking to someone. I think to myself I'm safe here, it's all over. It's probably just the police asking about the incident. Staring in the doc's direction, I see him and a man talking. Their backs are turned away from me. I don't see any police badges or anything. So now my mind is racing! The doctor begins to walk away, and the man turns toward me and there it was. That dirty smirk! How did he find me? Why are they giving him any info about me? Are they in on it? Or is this just a dream? As I close my eyes for a second and reopen them, I realize, no, this isn't a dream.

As the man approaches, my eyes widen. I'm scared to death. Why is this man so out too kill me? What is it that he wants from me? I hear voices coming from the nurses' station down the hall. I hear someone saying they were from the police department, asking to see the patient who was injured earlier! As their footsteps get louder, the man runs off down the other hallway. Now I have a face to go with the dirty smirk.

I try to tell the police and nurses that the man who did this was just in my room, but no one was listening. They wanted details of what happened earlier. I told them what I could recall. They told me to get some rest. Yeah, how am I going to rest with some crazy man trying to kill me?

I doze in and out of consciousness from the pain meds for the next day or so. I'm making a slow but steady recovery, and so far no return of the dirty smirk guy. He is a towering man, around 6'5" and 250 pounds with dark brown hair and a scruffy face and dark set eyes. Very well dressed for being an attempted murderer, I must say. Was this his way of hiding his real identity? I believe so.

Nobody here in the hospital nor in the outside world really knew much about me, and I like it that way. But this man must! I'm getting released from here today, not knowing if I'll make it home or not. I'm filled with fear, but what can I do? Hide my whole life? No! As I'm leaving the hospital, I search around every corner, every nook and cranny to make sure he isn't there! I don't see the man anywhere.

As I'm waiting for the cab to pick me up, I look around the vast parking lot to see if anyone is watching me. I can't see anything. It's too big to spot anyone watching me. I take a deep breath of the fresh summer air. Let out a big sigh. The cab is here so I get in and tell the man in front where I want to go. I take in the sights along the way. The stunning views of the river gently flowing down the hillside. The beautiful mountains that surround the area.

We come to a stop light, and as I'm looking around my town I'm seeing the hustle and bustle of the traffic and people. I think to myself, these people really don't know what they aren't seeing. Which is life. Then the man in the cab says something that snaps me back to reality.

"I know who you are."

Stunned, I said, "Excuse me."

"Oh, nothing. I was just thinking out loud."

Now thoughts were racing through my mind. Is this guy really thinking out loud? Or does he really know who I am? I keep my mouth shut, not pushing the issue any further.

We get to my place and I get out. I hand the man his money, and stand there waiting to see where he is going as he drives down the street until I can no longer see the vehicle. I go inside my little apartment, looking around, taking in everything like I had never been here before. A slight layer of dust has gathered on the coffee table and shelves. Too tired to really care, I sit on the sofa and kick off my shoes and stare at the black TV screen. I begin to get lost in my thoughts. Who are these people? What do they want? I sit on my sofa for a couple more hours trying to gather my thoughts.

I get up slowly and make my way to the kitchen to grab a soda and something to eat from the refrigerator. I sit down at the table with my lunch and think to myself what a lonely life I live. No family, no pets, and people trying to kill me! I eat my baloney sandwich and take a sip of my soda. As I'm sitting there trying to fully process the events from the past several days, I think to myself I have to find out who and what these people want from me!

I finish my dinner and decide to take a shower. Enjoying the warmth of the hot water trickling down my body and the fresh scent of the shampoo and soap, I just lose all of my worries for the next twenty minutes. I go to my room, shuffle through my clothes, and grab a decent t-shirt and pair of blue jeans and get dressed.

I hear what sounded like a knock on my door. I stand there for a few seconds and listen. There it is again. It is at my door. I head over to my closet and get out my safe box that I keep in the upper right hand corner of the closet. I get out my 9 mm Beretta. I slowly walk to the hallway from my bedroom that leads to the front door. I creep along like someone is already in here! I get to my door and peek through the peephole, expecting the worst. I see it's my old friend, Mark.

I lower the gun and put it on safety, unlock the door, and slowly open it.

"Mark. So glad to see you."

With a big smile on his face and tears in his eyes, he replies, "It's great to know your okay."

"How do you know what happened?"

He told me that there were some people we knew just down the street from where it happened, and that's how he knew.

Mark is a short but stocky kind of guy at 5'6 and 180, solid muscle, light sandy blonde hair, clean shaven. He is what they call a pretty boy. But don't let his looks fool you, the man can fight.

I quickly lose track of the whole part of being injured and being hunted like a rabid dog. I let him in. Not bringing up much about the whole incident, we start catching up on old times, then he asks, "How ya doin', man?"

"I'm here."

"What have you gotten yourself into?"

"What do you mean what have I gotten myself into? I don't know what these people want or how they know me."

With a small smirk on his face Mark says, "Yes, you do."

2

I've known Mark for the better part of twenty years. We went to grade school and all the way through college together. We even worked at a few places together. One in particular. Back in the early nineties, we worked for a mid-sized company in Colorado, Milford Law Firm. Mark and I worked for this company for several years. They had the most extravagant parties, and we got regular bonuses and pay raises. I'm not talking just a $1,000 to a $2,000 dollar bonus. I'm talking $10,000 bonus plus pay raises every couple months.

You see, we were just starting our careers as criminal defense attorneys. Mark and I mostly handled the small cases such as little punks who couldn't leave the drugs alone or the woman beaters who should've been locked up anyway. At times, I often wondered why I chose to be a criminal defense attorney in the first place.

Over time we worked our way to some of the bigger cases, like some of the lower legs of the mob. It was kind of funny to see some of these guys act like they were important until their mob boss would come in and slap them around a little bit. In 1992,

Mark and I finally cracked a couple big cases for the firm. In return we got some of the higher profile cases with some of the mob bigwigs. From that point on, we had all the access we needed to any of the firm's files.

Mark and I began to wonder how the firm was able to give these high bonuses and pay raises. Sure, they had some big-time clients, but not that many. We began to listen and watch at parties and such for any clue. But it wasn't until we decided to dig into their records when we found out they were robbing these clients blind, and not just the clients but other people as well.

We weren't always so supportive of the people we represented, but we were making money. Our company dealt with anything from lawsuits to mobsters. Little did we know, our boss was a low-life mobster himself! We dug through files and the boss's office desk drawer. What we found in his desk was his little black book and a disk that had no labeling. I took everything I could find. We rummaged through the files and took copies of the files and then returned the files the next day. I didn't return the disk but instead replaced it with a blank one. They would never know the difference unless they looked at it.

"The Boss," also known as Frank Milford to outsiders, was in his mid forties. He was a slender man, with dark brown hair, weighed 150 pounds if he was lucky, and he wore glasses. He wasn't the suit and tie kind of guy. He was a kind man, or so we thought.

We knew that returning the files wasn't going to be easy as the boss was in his office all day long. And let's not forget his sidekick, Edward. So we had to come up with a distraction. Mark would call the boss out to his desk and make up some type of crazy idea he had for getting new clients for the company. Edward wasn't always in the office, but when he was you knew not to go anywhere near the boss or the office. So we would make sure Edward was gone for the day so I could sneak in and replace the files.

After a couple of weeks, we gathered a lot of information. When I went to replace the last couple of files in his office, I got caught by Edward.

"Hey, what are you doing with the files?" said this 6'2", 280-pound balding gorilla.

It was Edward! I about jumped out of my pants because it came as a complete surprise. Trying to gather my thoughts, I quickly say while stuffing the files back into the file cabinet, "I was just looking for one of my client's file."

"You know you're not to be getting into the boss's files. Now get out of here!"

Well, I'm not going to argue with a man twice my size and with his record. I quickly remove myself out of the office.

I go find Mark at his desk and tell him that I was caught in the act. I see Edward and the boss through his window having a discussion about me getting into his files. How did I know this? Because Edward pointed right at me.

The boss came out and yelled, "Joe, get in here."

I looked at Mark as if to say, "Help."

Mark looked back at me and said, "Just play it cool, man."

"Yeah, easy for you too say."

I head to the boss's office. He closed the door behind me and said, "Have a seat." I sit down, and he continued, "Joe, I've known you for a couple years now. You and Mark are good employees, but what were you doing with *my* files?"

"Just looking for one of my client's files."

"Is that all?"

I said yes. He takes a long deep breath and then lets out a big sigh, his eyes glued to me like a hawk focused on his prey. He said, "Okay, go back to work."

The man didn't have a harsh voice, more of a fatherly type. Kind and caring, even when he is scolding someone. He wouldn't scare a mouse. Watching him from my desk, I saw him and Edward talking. I was wondering what they were saying, although I had a vague idea and so did Mark. We both decided that we better do what we were going to do and do it fast.

We went home for the day. I told Mark to meet me at my place at seven that night. On my way home, I looked over my shoulder to make sure Edward wasn't following me. No sign of him. I knew that the boss and Edward both knew I wasn't just in the office looking for a client's file. Mark showed up at seven and we started to go through the files, piecing it together.

I said to Mark, "We have enough here to hang these guys, let's get it to the police tonight."

Mark replies, "I don't want no part of this, man."

"Well, it's too late for that, you already are."

He said if I wanted to turn this in I was on my own. He didn't want these guys coming after him. After a heated discussion, I looked at Mark and said, "I'm going to the police tonight! With or without you. It's your choice, but we started this thing together, we should finish it together."

Mark left without saying a word. Needless to say, I turned in the files I had against the company.

It took the county's attorney's office a couple of months to build a solid case against them. After a complete investigation the boss and Edward and many others were arrested. I didn't really keep up with the case and moved on, or so I thought. Was it the boss and Edward coming after me after all these years? Were they released from prison? It seems so.

After a nice visit with Mark, he decides to leave for home. As he walks out the door, he turns to me and says, "Take care of yourself."

Really not wanting my best friend to leave and that little bit of security I had with him being around, I say, "I will." Knowing it's not going to do me any good to live my life in fear.

3

The next morning, I decide I would go for a walk through town to see what's going on in the real world. I get up the next morning. The sun is shining, birds are chirping, and I can hear the hustle and bustle of the traffic below. In the back of my mind I wonder if it is a good idea to leave the comfort and safety of my apartment. I decided it is for my sanity and other reasons. So I put on one of my favorite St. Louis Rams jacket and head downstairs to the street. Without even thinking about what has happened or who might be after me, I decide I want to walk up to one of the streams just on the outskirts of town. It's a Saturday morning. A beautiful one, I must say.

As I walk down the sidewalk past a couple of the local bakery shops, I get a whiff of freshly baked homemade cinnamon rolls. I stop and grab one for my walk. There is a beautiful gal who works in the bakery and she happens to be working today. As I enter the bakery, the little doorbell rings. She has her back turned away from the door and I can see her dark flowing hair as she turns to see who came in. She smiles, and what a smile she has. And those hazel green eyes are to die for.

"Hi, Joe. How are you?"

I reply shyly and say, "I'm doing okay."

Her name is Annie, and she owns the bakery. It's a neat little setup. The bakery has that fifties diner feel to it, with the old diner bench seats that are a light pink and the old diner tables and on each of the tables are perfectly placed table clothes. Every table also has its own centerpiece with the scent of freshly picked flowers and the smell of the homemade rolls, cookies, and other goodies. It's like you have died and went to heaven. I've had a crush on Annie for awhile and I think the feeling is mutual but I just never had the nerve to ask her out. She is single but I just didn't feel it was the right time.

"What can I get you today, Joe?"

"One of those good smelling cinnamon rolls."

She lightly giggles and reaches in the glass cabinet and places it in a container for me. "That will be 2.50, please"

I hand her the money, smile, and say, "Thank you!" I continue on my way to my destination.

I reach the stream after about a fifteen-minute walk. I sit down on an old picnic table that looks pretty worn. Some of the boards are rotten and it looks as though some of the bolts are missing and it could use a paint job and a good sealing. I open my container to eat that big cinnamon roll. I take my first bite and it melts in my mouth. The frosting isn't rich but just right, still warm and gooey the way I like 'em.

You can smell the fresh cut grass and the fresh water from the stream. I take in a deep breath of the summer air. It's so refreshing.

It's like smelling a freshly bloomed rose. I hear children playing in the park which runs along the bank of the stream. I finish my roll, get up, and decide to go over and check out the stream. The stream is so clear that you can see the trout swimming along. Man, I wish I would have gotten my pole and license this year. Not like I could cast a line anyway. I'm not fully healed yet, but maybe in a week or two.

I continue to head down the little trail. The kids' laughter and the sounds of the squeaky swings fill the air with calm and serenity. I sit down on a bench away from where the kids are playing and take in the sights of the beautiful snowcapped mountains in the background. There isn't a cloud in the sky and not a worry in my head. I sit here for an hour or so just taking in the fresh air, the laughter of the kids, and background noise of the stream gently flowing past me.

I then decide to head back toward town to see what is happening around there. As I'm walking, I get a glimpse of a man sitting along the south side of the road looking toward my direction, staring at me like he was going to jump out of his car and kick my rear I looked back at the man to see if he was going to do something. I couldn't make any eye contact with the man or know for sure if he was looking at me because he had shades on. I would say from the looks of him he was probably around 5'11" and 170 pounds or so. He had light grayish-brown hair, a black t-shirt, and a rather large frame.

I just continued to watch for him to make his move. The children in the background are still laughing and playing on the swing set, then all of a sudden the man jumps out of his car. I freeze in fear that he was coming after me. I'm so tense, my muscles start to ache. I clench my fist as he gets closer to me ready to defend myself. The man is now right in front of me. He looks at me and says, "Relax, man, I'm just going to get my kid!" I relax my fist and kinda give the man a nod and let out a deep sigh. Man, you really got to quit being so paranoid, not everyone is out to get you.

I continue on my way into town. It's probably around three in the afternoon. I figure there is a little restaurant in the mall that serves the best Mexican food around and since I totally spaced off lunch, I'm starved. On my way into town, you can hear the birds chirping in the background, the sounds of the cars passing you by, and the warmth of the sun beating down on me.

Across the street is the old auto parts store ran by one of my old neighbors, Mr. Thompson. He ran the store for many years and was always cleaning and straightening the products on the shelves. I could remember always going in and saying hi to him then once in a while I would move something out of its place just to see what he would do. He would calmly say to me, "Dang it, Joe, I swear you just do stuff like that to make me work," with a smile on his face.

There is a couple of old abandoned buildings on the north side of the street that used to be booming with business. Now it's like an old ghost town. I can't recall the names of them or what they sold there, but I wish they would get a new company in to open the stores back up. The buildings are still in great shape. Just a new round of paint would make them look new again.

I continue on down the street and see the old movie theater that's been closed for years now. As a kid I would go there every weekend to catch a flick with Mark and a couple of our friends. The awning is all torn and should be torn down and the windows are busted out They had the old wood doors where you would enter and exit from. The paint has chipped away and a small pile has gathered beneath the doors. I walk past the town square, just a big round circle with a playground for the kids to play on and some benches. In the center is a big old fountain and on the outer perimeter is a huge flower bed with all kinds of flowers, from rose bushes to tulips. The colors are very vibrant, reds oranges, yellows, pinks. It's gorgeous and very well maintained.

I finally reach the mall and walk over to the Mexican restaurant. I go to the counter and order me a smothered burrito with some green chili sauce. I go sit at a table in the back of the restaurant and wait for my number to be called. As I'm sitting there, I look around at the people shopping, laughing, and looking through clothes and whatever else they could find. I just take in the moment of someone else's life and their happiness that they share with their friends and loved ones. I kinda chuckle to myself. Why am I not just living day to day like everyone else?

The mall has everything in it. There is a candy shop, jewelry stores, game rooms, clothing stores, and anything else you could think of. The floors are a dark marble with a hint of a light brown in it. At Christmas time, they put a thirty-feet tree in the middle of the mall, decorate it, and when it's done it is beautiful. One year I sat here on a bench for at least two hours just looking at the tree. They also place presents under the tree for the less fortunate kids and it's such a joy to see their faces light up when they receive those gifts!

Breaking my train of thought, I hear the guy at the counter yell out my number. I go to the counter and get my plate. You can see the steam rolling off the burrito. The green chili rolls off the edges of this huge thing. Cheese is melted over the top and you get a slight hint of the refried beans and the seasonings that made it smell delicious.

I walk over to the condiments, grab some sour cream and a little hot sauce, and wander back over to my table and sit down. If you've ever had real Mexican food, you know that they have rice, refried beans, and their beef isn't ground but shredded. Well, I've eaten in some restaurants that had smothered burritos, and you would spend hours just chewing on the meat itself. That's not enjoyable, but these guys, everything just melts in your mouth.

I finish my meal and wander out of the restaurant. I decide to go check out some of the gift shops and sports shops. I find some wind pants and a couple of jerseys I want to get so I take them up to the counter, pay for them, and head out of the mall.

4

I should really head home to do some light cleaning of the apartment. I slowly walk down the sidewalk making my way toward home. I get there and I take the elevator. I'm too lazy for the stairs right now. I get to my floor, get off the elevator, and go to my door. I place the key into the key slot, turn it, and swing open the door. I place my bags by the couch and close the door, then I take my jacket off and hang it on the hook next to the door.

I turn toward the couch, grab the remote sitting on the back left side corner where I always leave it, turn on the TV, and walk around and have a seat on the couch to take my shoes off. I flip through the channels. There's nothing good on really, so I just sit the remote on the coffee stand and kick off my shoes. I look around the apartment, not really having the ambition to clean. I just sit back, kick my feet up on the coffee table, and fall asleep.

Suddenly I'm awakened by a loud banging on my door. I jump, rub my eyes, and go to the door to see who is there. I see badges. Still not fully awake, I open the door and see two men dressed in police uniforms. Both of the men stood around six feet tall and of medium weight. If I had to guess, they are probably around 180 or so.

The man to my right was an old man. You could see the grey throughout his mustache and sideburns. He has some hints of freckles on his face and has light blue eyes. The officer to my left was clean shaven, in his mid-thirties, with brown hair and brown eyes. Their uniforms were neatly tucked in and no wrinkles anywhere. Their shoes shined like they had just been polished, and their ties are placed perfectly on their chest.

I ask how I can help them.

Joe Mieser, one of the officers, says, "We need you to come down to the police station. We think we caught your guy and we need you to identify him. We will wait here for you and give you a ride downtown."

I'm staring at the two officers, wondering why the hell they woke me up. I go grab my shoes and keys, close and lock the door behind me. On the way downtown sitting in the back of the police cruiser, I think maybe this part of my life is over and I can move on with my life without always looking over my shoulders.

We arrive at the station. I am still kinda groggy. The officers tell me they were going to show me six men. I should pick the one I recognize from the lineup.

The men walk into the room side by side. They turn the lights on and have them step up one by one so I can get a real good look at their faces. The first man was about 5'6" or maybe 5'7", balding, and looks like he has never shaven in his entire life. Also, the man had a slight limp on his right side. The man looked like he had been hit by a Mack truck a couple times. His face looks like an old rock that has been exposed to the weather for many years. You could see the creases and every wrinkle in his face. His eyes looks like they could tell you a story of a lifetime. You could tell life has beaten the poor man down but yet he fights on.

The second man is a tall, dark male, with short curly hair, standing about 6'5", well dressed. He has dark eyes. He is younger, couldn't be much more than thirty or so and clean shaven. I would have almost thought they went to the bank and dragged the poor man out of his office. I get to the last guy, look him over good.

I say to the police officers, "It's none of these guys."

"Are you sure?"

I said positive. The two officers tell me not to worry, that they will find the man who attacked me. They took me back to my apartment.

5

I get in the elevator, push the button for the second floor where my apartment is. I'm filled with disappointment that the man wasn't caught, and I am faced with the reality that he is still gonna come for me. I get to my floor. My door way is about five steps to the right of the elevator. As the door opens, I glance toward my door. I see it's cracked open. I headed over to the door when I hear voices coming from my apartment.

I hear one man say, "Shhh, someone just got off the elevator."

I take off running as quiet and as quickly as I can. I hide around the corner. I hear another man's voice.

"No one is here. Must have been a neighbor. Keep looking."

The only form of protection I have is in my closet. I now have pieced it together. These men must have been hired by my old boss to get rid of me and the files.

I kept copies of all the files in case of any mishaps. I never returned the disk and I never looked at it, so there must be something that is still very damning to him, and I'm sure to

Edward as well. I do know that all the charges against my old boss and Edward didn't stick and they are up for parole in 2014.

I stand quiet in the hallway, trying not to give up my position, praying that they hurry up and leave, but they keep going through my stuff. Then I hear another man's voice.

"Let's go."

I remember that voice well. Edwards.

"Let's go, we will come back later," he says to the other two men.

I stay hidden around the corner and wait to see if they take the elevator or head for the stairs. I hear the ding of the elevators door and it opens then closes. Dreading the thought of having to peek around the corner to see if they were gone or not, I slowly poke my head around the corner inch by inch until I can see.

I don't see anybody so I step out into the hallway facing my apartment. I start slowly walking toward it. I get to my door. I hear and see nothing coming from my place. I push the door and proceed in checking around for anyone who may still be there. Nothing. My place is torn up, like a tornado hit it. Papers on the floor, drawers thrown around. My couch is flipped over. Clothes all over the place. I better get my gun, I'm going to need it.

I go to my closet to retrieve my safe but it's not there. I start to look around to see if it was around my room and I find it on the other side of my bed. They have cracked it open. My gun isn't there, they must've thought I had stuff in that safe but I wasn't that dumb to keep that kind of stuff at home.

Now I'm completely defenseless, and I know they are going to be back to finish what they have started. I have no doubt that they will stop at nothing to get what they are after, even if that means going after people I know and care about. What am I going to do? Yeah, I can contact the police department, but what good is that going to do? They seem to be a step ahead of the police, and if I run they are going to do something to my friends and others who I love and care about. Well, whatever it is, I better think of it fast, because I know Edward and he is a man of his word. They will be back tonight.

Staying in the apartment is not an option, especially when trying to fight for your life. I sit in my mess of a home, not even worrying about cleaning it up. I come up with a plan. I grab a piece of paper and write a note to Mr. Edward.

> Well, hello, Edward. Nice to see you are out of prison and decided to come pay me a visit. How did you find me? Oh, it really doesn't matter does it? I have what you want but you're going to have to play it my way for now. I'll meet you at the old abandoned concrete building on the south side of town Monday night around 10 p.m. with what you want.

I know they are going to kill me but it keeps them away from anybody I know. I kept all the files and the disk in a safe box at the bank so no one could get to I post the note on the door of my apartment I don't even bother to lock up when I left as they would just get in anyway. I have packed a few items that I was going to need.

6

The next morning I head to the bank and retrieve the items in the lock box. As I leave the bank, I head to the motel down the street. It's not the best of places to stay but it will do for now. Now to sit and wait, knowing that I'm probably being watched. I don't dare go to anyone I know to seek refuge as that will put them in harm's way.

I get to the motel and check in at the front desk. There is a lady with a dark blue dress on with her name badge neatly placed on the left side of her chest. The name reads Jessica. She greets me with a smile and welcomes me to Pines Inn. I tell her I needed to rent a room for a couple of days. She enters my info into the computer and then swipes my key to the room through the card read to activate it and hands me the key. I smile and tell her thank you.

There is a sign with directions to reach the rooms. The main lobby has a red carpet and old-style furniture with a cabin feel to it. The decor and the carpet doesn't really match the cabin style. You can tell that it hasn't been updated to what it should be. The walls have wainscoting on the bottom and wallpaper from the mid-sixties, it looks like. I walk down the hall to reach the stairs to go to my room, 162. I get to the top of the stairs, read the sign, and turn to my right and head down to the end of the hall. 162, that's me. I place the key into the key reader so I can get into the room. At first it wouldn't open. Noticing that I had the key turned the wrong way, I turn it around and slide it through again. This time it works! I open the door, come into the room, sit my bag down, and look around.

The same decor as downstairs is up here as well, minus the ugly red carpet. I have grey carpet. The room has a slight hint of that old musty smell. You know, like when a house hasn't been occupied for awhile. I open the window a hair to get some fresh air in for a little bit. I go through my bag and rummaged through the files. I need to know what is on this disc. The motel does offer internet services but there is no computer here in my room. I'll have to go down to the lobby later and see if they have one I can use. I grab the remote off the nightstand on the right side of the bed. I turn on the TV to try to distract myself for a little while, then I decide I better get to thinking about how I am going to deal with the little problem I have.

I'm tired of running and hiding, but my biggest fear is to put others in harm's way I couldn't stay at my apartment and stand my ground there, too many people, so it's going to go down at the old concrete plant. But for now it's time just to relax.

An hour or two has passed. I decide that I should go down to the front desk and ask see if there is a computer I could use. I pick up the files, place them back into my bag, and grab the disc off the stand and head downstairs. I get to the front desk and ask the lady if there were any computers for the public to use. She said to go down the hallway to the end, take a left, go three doors down, and to the left there is a computer in there I can use!

I thank her and head down the hallway, still looking at the old decor in kind of a dismay. Why would anyone keep it looking like this? I reach the end, turn to my left, and go three doors down to where the computer is. I walk into the room and see the computer. There is an old chair in front of the desk that looks like it is at least a hundred years old. I'm almost scared to sit in it. I grab ahold of it and inspect it before I decide to sit down. It looks to be a sound chair regardless of its appearance.

I sit and scoot myself closer to the computer, turn it on, then wait for the screen to turn on. When it does I place the disc into the slot and wait for it to show me what to do next. To my surprise I don't have to do anything. The documents pop up and what is on there shocks me even more than I thought it would. Records of millions of dollars from people that have been targets of fraud and embezzlement. As I keep digging into the disc, I see that they have even kept records of murders, drug deals, and big purchases of large amounts of weapons. They also have contacts with some of the known terrorist groups overseas. I pop out the disc and quickly realize this is bigger than what I had ever thought.

I cannot let these guys get their hands on this disc. Instead of going back to my room, I shove the disc in my back pocket and head back toward the lobby and out the front door. I head down the street to the bank, maybe three or four blocks away.

Once there, I ask to get a safe deposit box and place the disc in it and close and lock it. I hand it back to the lady and she takes it to the back of the bank and puts it into a slot and closes the door behind her. She walks back to me and asks if there was anything else she could do for me. I tell the lady no. I head back over to the motel and go back to my room. As seconds turn into minutes and minutes turn into hours, the clock isn't my friend as time ticks away. As one day passes, a new one began.

    I start to piece together my plan of survival and finally I have it all played out in my head. Whether or not it will work is another thing.

7

It's now Sunday, one day before showdown. After living on delivery for a couple of days now and hiding from the rest of the world, I'm starting to go insane but my concentration is on tomorrow night. I know the ins and outs of the old plant. My father was a foreman there for many years and I used to visit him often while he was working. So that is the perfect place to do this, plus I know every escape route where they won't which is a huge bonus for me.

It's a nice sunny day. The sun peeks through my curtains in the motel room. I pull open the curtains and open the window to let some fresh air in. There is a slight breeze flowing through the motel room. I can hear the birds singing and the Sunday morning traffic buzzing by after church. You can also hear the church bells dinging in the distance. I decide to step out on the little balcony off of my room. It's a little area where if I wanted to just take a chair out and sit I could, and I just may do that. Besides, no one is going to try to kill me until the get what they want.

SUMMER NITES

I stand there watching the birds flying carefree in the sky and the listen to the sounds around me, lost in the moment of the carefree world around me. I see people walking down the sidewalk. They look up and see me standing there. They smile and wave as they pass by. I wave back to them. I run my hand across my face feeling the scruff that has grown the past couple of days. I step back into the room, grab my night bag, reach in, and pull out the razor and shaving cream from my travelers' kit and go to the bathroom sink. I turn on the hot water, grab the shaving cream, give it a good shake, and then lather my face. I rinse my hand off to get rid of any of the excess shaving cream and then grab my razor and begin to remove the hair from my face. I feel much better after getting that itchy long hair off.

I take a look in the mirror. I don't really ever look at myself in mirrors, or anything else for that matter. I stand at around 5'11", 160 pounds, medium build, blue eyes, and light brown hair about neck length. I stare into the mirror for a few minutes longer. I don't know why but I do. I reach down with my hands cupped together, get some water in my hands, and splash it on my face. I reach over and grab one of the towels the maid had dropped off earlier. The fresh scent of lavender laundry detergent filled the room. I dried off my face and hands, turned off the faucet, and walked out to the living area. I sit on the bed and just take everything in. Is this going to be the last time I see the sun shining, hear the birds chirping and sounds of the cars as they drive down the street, the sweet laughter of the kids playing in the park, the warm breeze of the summer air, the fresh smell of the summer rain? I hope not. I decide I'm going to go for a walk. I'm not going to pay attention to the clock or the fact that this could be my last day on earth. I'm just going to go enjoy the day. I head uptown toward the town park with a big water fountain that sits in the center of town. It is very peaceful to sit and listen to the water splashing into the pond below. It's only about three blocks from the motel where I'm staying.

I walk up to the bench that sits about three feet away from the fountain and I take a seat. The kids like to run around it and throw pennies in the pond to make their wish. You can feel the cool mist from it as you sit there by the fountain. Some people don't like it. I rather enjoy it. I sit there, soak up the sun, and watch the children as they run around and play and giggle at each other.

After about an hour I decide to get up and go wander around the streets of town for awhile longer. I go past the bakery and glance through the window. I stop and stare in as I see Annie standing at the counter helping a customer. I'm lost in her beauty and just stare at her. She glances in my direction, see's me looking at her, and she kind of grins at me. Embarrassed, I quickly leave the scene of the crime. I didn't want her to think I was a weirdo, since I was lost in her beauty.

I regret now that I have not gotten the courage to ask her on a date. Who knows where it could have gone? I guess I'll never know. I continue on my little stroll around town just checking stuff out then decide I better get back to the motel.

Later that evening, as I sit thinking about things, my nerves begin to kick in. I try to distract myself by turning on the radio and then the TV. Nothing seemed to be working. I began thinking to myself. I'm in this alone, no one to stand beside me. What had started out as two friends working on this together to put some bad people in their place ends up with me on the receiving end of the whole mess.

Then I got to thinking more about Mark. Why did he back away from the whole deal? Was he really that scared and wanted no part of it? Mark lives hundreds of miles away from me. The boss had no clue Mark had anything to do with this. He really did, but just the distraction part of it. And how would they have found me here? Of course I didn't really move away either. But they still had no clue on my whereabouts. Unless they had someone close to me tell them.

Mark and I didn't talk much after the blowup over the whole thing. Matter of fact, it had been years. Sure we had friends in the area but none would have told anybody except the ones close by what had happened. Trying not to think that a friend of many years would have possibly betrayed me, I shift my thoughts back to getting rest for the big day, but once again it's odd that he shows, disappears, and then I have Edward and his goons show up at my apartment. They have to have someone on the inside who would know my whereabouts.

I lay down on my bed. It's time to get some sleep, but the thought keeps running through my mind. Did my best friend betray me? If so, why? Was he being paid by the boss to help them get their little revenge on me for stealing their files and turning them in? Or was Mark in on it the whole time? Because he knew I wasn't the type to just turn my head and look the other way when I knew things weren't right and I have always been that way.

Mark had always been the risk taker. He needs excitement in his life or he isn't satisfied, but I wouldn't think he would do something like this. As I lay there in the bed watching the sun slowly start to disappear behind the mountains, I slowly drift in and out of sleep. I toss and turn throughout the night. I roll over one last time, look at the clock which reads 4 a.m. Frustrated, I throw a pillow off the other side of the bed, grab the remote, turn the TV on again, and try to find something entertaining.

It's now Monday morning. The day will drag on with the plan in my head on how to survive this and the thought that maybe my best friend could be in on the whole mess. I try not to think of what will be. I flip through the channels and finally find some mindless comedy show. I'm lost in the TV and pay no attention to what's around me just, focused on the TV. I watch TV for an hour or two then decide to go take a nice hot shower and get ready for the day. I get done with my shower, get dressed, and gather everything I'm going to need for tonight.

8

I hear a knock on the door. Probably just the housekeeper coming to get the laundry. I get to the door, peek through the peephole, and indeed it was the maid. I grabbed the dirty towels, open the door, and hand her the laundry and give her a smile and a small tip.

I close the door and walk over to the nightstand where there is a phone. I pick up the telephone and call room services. I order a couple of flap Jacks and some orange juice although the motel don't serve lunch or dinner they have a mean breakfast menu. I finish placing my order and place the phone back down. I wait for the arrival of my food. While waiting, I go over to the window and draw back the curtains.

There is a slight haze over the town and off in the distance you can see the sun dancing in and out of the clouds. I can still feel the warmth of the sun through the window pane I slide the window open a hair so some fresh air can come through the room. I go back over to the bed and sit down and stare at the TV. There's nothing really on but it distracts me enough not to let my nerves get the best of me.

There is another knock on my door. "Room service," I hear the man say.

I get up off the bed, head over to the door, open it, and the small frail young man with glasses and uniform says to me, "Good morning, Mr. Mieser. I have your order for you."

I tell him thank you and grab the tray and tell him to hold on a second. I put the tray down on the dress and grab my wallet and pull out a five-dollar bill and walk back to the door and hand it to the young man. I said here you go have a good day! I close my door and lock it and grab a chair and pull it over to the little stand and sit down.

I pull off the lid to the tray. There are three huge flapjacks with chopped-up bananas covering the top and covering the bananas is a light layer of strawberry syrup. I take my first bite of the flapjacks and the sweet taste of the strawberry syrup mixed with the bananas on the flapjack is awesome. They just melt in your mouth. I quickly devour the flapjacks, wipe my mouth with the napkin, place the lid back on the tray, and just kick back.

As I'm relaxing, the thought of Mark being in on this crosses my mind once again. If he is, it poses a big problem as he knows the old concrete plant as well as I do. As the day proceeds, I decide to grab a jacket and walk to the old plant so I can plan a route of escape and to see where the best place would be to lure these guys. Mark may know the layout of the old plant but many parts of it is crumbling and he hasn't been here in years to know what I know.

I walk down the street to Jefferson Street, hang a right, and head down to the old plant. There are some old buildings around the old plant. The old lumberyard is just to the east. They closed it down back in 2000 but someone from out of state came in and bought it and has been doing some renovation. To the southeast, there is an old crumbling building about two or three blocks away. They should have demolished that years ago, but yet it still stands. Off to the southwest, there are open fields with wildflowers growing all over the place. Soon those felids won't be there. They are wanting to develop it for more housing and more stores.

I get to the old plant and look around the grounds. There is an old pickup that sits old and rusting in the background. You can see on the east side of the building that parts of the walls are starting to fall down there are pieces of the cement wall piled up along the edge of the first floor wall.

There used to be an old elevator that would take you up and down to each floor. It would be a huge risk to use it because of the unstableness of the building, but I would use it if need be. The power is still on because the city didn't want turned it off due to the fact they had people who came and checked for squatters and it would be too big of a risk for them even with a flashlight to go in. I wander to the south side of the building. The plant has four doors, one on each side of the plant for emergency exits. I want to make sure they are all clear so I can use any one of them at anytime. The door on the south side is clear of any debris. There are tools all over the ground that past employees have just left.

Hammers, wires, pliers, shovels, gloves, you name it, it's here. Keeping that in mind because that will give me some kind of defense, I wandered over to the west side of the building and look around. Part of this side of the building has collapsed as well but the door is clear. All the windows in the building has been broken out. Good thing it's summer I won't freeze. I walk back to the front of the building checking every part of it to find any possible way out of here I can get.

I enter through the front door of the building. You can hear the flapping of wings and cooing of the pigeons inside. The floor is covered with concrete dust and pieces of rubble from the upper floors collapsing. Rays of sunshine through the broken windows, and at least there is some fresh air flowing in. You can look down the hall and see where the old offices are. I know them all very well. I used to run in and out of this old place for years. I want to go to the fifth floor, a wide open area with columns throughout, so I could take cover. It also has a little storage spot in the southeast corner that I can hide a few items in.

The first floor is where most of the equipment is. There still is some old conveyors and some rope. I go and pick up the rope, look it over. It's about a hundred foot with no frays. I can use this. In the corner I see some old poles that might come in handy too. I take the rope with me. I walk back toward the hallway and continue to the stairs. As I walk past the offices I look through each window. All the desks and chairs are still there covered with layers of dust. Pictures still hang on the walls as well as old calendars. Nothing of use, but it brings memories back. I get to the door of the stairs. There is a small window so you can see what's on the other side. There is a pile of concrete from up above that has settled behind the door. This may be a task to get open, but I have to try to shove it open but it won't move. I step back a little bit and try to ram my way through the door. I maybe got it to move an inch if I'm lucky I have to come up with a plan to get through this door.

The elevator is just a couple steps away to my left. I can try to see if it will work or not. There is a breaker box down to the right of the elevator, so I walk over, open the panel, and flip the breakers to the on position. Closing the panel door, I turn back toward the elevator. This stuff hasn't ran in years, so I'm not going to hold my breath and not too mention it is a huge risk, even if it does work.

I get back over to the elevator. I see the lights are on for the up and down buttons. I suck in a deep breath of air holding it in and push the button. I hear the machine come to life releasing my breath and with a whisper of a yes! Under my breath, I hear the elevator creaking down the shaft and the doors open. I am amazed by only seeing just layers of dust in there and not boulders. I step inside.

I'm not too sure I want the door to close. I stand there holding the open button so the doors will not close. Finally, I release the button; the door closes, and I feel a slight jolt from it engaging. You could hear the grumbles of the cables as they lift the elevator up to the second floor.

I feel a sudden stop when I reach the second floor. The door opens slowly, then I realize that I should've grabbed one of the shovels from outside because I had no way to clear the rubble away from the door when I got to it. I push the first floor button and the door closes. I think to myself if I keep this up things will not go well for me.

I reach the first floor. Once again the door opens. I step out, not concerned of anyone being in the building. I head back to the main door to retrieve the shovel. I get to the door, push it open, walk to the south side of the building, and grab the shovel and a hammer, and then I see a utility knife sticking out of an old tool box. I grab it and a pair of pliers as well. The blade will come in handy for cutting stuff like the rope. I head back inside and get back into the elevator to the second floor. I get to the second floor and again the door opens. I step out and there is bird crap everywhere, but I can't worry about that. I need to get this stuff done. Time is slipping away. I head toward the small corner of the northwest part of the second floor where the access to the stairs are. I look through the window to see if I can get through there or not and to make sure there was still a set of stairs there.

 It's clear. I open the door and it makes a loud creaking noise as I push it open. The stairs are in rough shape but passable. I head down the flight of stairs. It's dark but I can still make out where I'm going. I finally reach the first floor. With shovel in hand I begin to move the debris away from the door. After about thirty minutes of scooping, I get the doorway clear and realize quickly how out of shape I really am.

 But there is no time to play around. As time ticks away, so do the chances of my survival. I head back up the stairs, not stopping at the second floor but checking every flight up to the fifth floor to make sure everything is okay and I can get to where I need to be freely and without causing injury to myself.

 I hurry and gather all the stuff I need and get it set up into place. I head back down to the first floor by stairs, not wanting to mess with the elevator to much in case I need it later. I go through the first floor door. I walk over to the panel where the breakers are and turn them off. I head back toward the front door, kind of soaking in some of the past memories of when my father and several of his old friends worked here.

SUMMER NITES

I walk back to my motel room, sit down on the edge of the bed. I better gather things and get prepared for a long night because these guys are not going to just leave me alone after they get what they want. I know too much about them and what they have done. They won't stop until I am dead.

9

The clock slowly ticks away. The sun is slowly fading into the background and all I can do is run my plans through my mind of what I need to do and how I'm going to do it. I want to get to the plant before Edward and his clowns do; otherwise, I cannot execute anything to save myself. I start thinking if I walk into this thing with no weapon, there is no chance of any survival.

There is a gun shop down on main street about a half mile from where my motel is. I know that Edward is going to have someone out watching for me but they can't do anything in the open so I get up off the bed and grab my jacket and head out the door. Hoping it's not too late and they haven't closed the store yet. I hurry downtown watching to see if I'm being followed by anyone. I reach the store and the bright neon sign says open. I go inside. There is a heavyset balding man at the counter smiling.

He says, "Hi, Joe, what can I do for you?"

I smile back, hiding my fears from him. "Hey, Bob, how are you?"

"Great, thanks for asking. What are we looking for tonight?" Bob asks.

"I want a 9 mm Beretta and a couple of clips with a lot of ammo."

Bob chuckles and says, "What, are you taking on an army?"

I laugh a little bit and say, "No, I just want to do some practicing."

"I see. So, how have you been? Have you fully healed from the accident?"

"I'm good, and yes it's healed nicely. It's still kind of tender but I can deal with that," I say with a smile.

"I'm glad to hear that. Is there anything else I can get for you?"

As I'm gazing around, I reply, "Maybe make that two of those nines and a couple holsters."

"Coming right up."

I pay Bob what I owed him. He tells me to be safe out there!

"I sure will."

10

There is a slight breeze but the stars are out and the moon is shining bright. I head back to my motel and gather everything I need. Everything is where it should be. I grab the clips and the ammo and start to load the clips. I'm very handy with these types of guns. I slide the clips into the Berettas and slip the holsters on. I glance over at the clock and it reads 7:30 p.m. I'll head over to the plant at 8:30, that way I can get there and get everything set up. The last hour goes by fast. I sit at the table, grab a pen and piece of paper, and write a note so it can be found by the maid telling them where I have gone and what was happening. I know more than likely they will not find the note until the following morning.

> To whom it may concern:
>
> This is Joe Mieser. I'm letting you know I am meeting with some very dangerous people tonight at 10:00 p.m. at the old concrete plant. More than

likely I will be dead when you get this. Please notify
the police if I do not return.

I grab the key to my room, lay the note on the bed, and grab the little backpack that I use for things like this. I walk out my door and head to the front desk and turn my key in to the attendant.

She smiles and asks, "Checking out?"

I say yes.

"Well, thank you, Mr. Mieser. We do appreciate your staying here."

"Thanks for the hospitality."

I head to the front door, push it open, step outside, and take a deep breath of fresh air. I began to walk down the street toward the plant. I get around the corner and turn toward the old crumbling plant. No lights are on. The place is deserted by the people who once worked there. The air is warm and the sky is clear, but my heart is pounding like thunder in the sky. I hurry to reach the building so I can get inside before anyone shows up.

The town does have some hidden secrets at night. The people of the streets come out to play. What I mean by the people of the streets is that we have our problems with drugs and prostitution, just like any bigger city. Then we have the forgotten people who linger in the night and hide throughout the day Along my way I see some of the forgotten ones digging through the trash cans for a bit to eat and on the streets begging for money. I pass one of the guys as I turn the corner and stop, turn to him, hand him some cash, and tell him go get something to eat and drink. He thanks me and rushes down the back streets.

I get to the main entrance of the door, pull it open, and make my way through the door. I look around, of course with a flashlight. I see nothing moving. It's very quiet. I head over to the hallway so I can make my way up to the fifth floor. Then I hear what sounds to be a door creaking open. I think to myself there is no way they could have gotten here before I did. I get to the door that leads upstairs. I'm kind of sprinting up them. I stop at each flight to listen for anymore sounds. I hear nothing. I finally reach the fifth floor. I swing open the door and proceed with caution, turning and searching every nook and cranny.

Nothing is there so I get to a spot where I want to be and won't be seen until I am ready. I look at my watch. It's now 9:45, they will be here any minute. I prepare myself for what's to come and once again the thought of Mark and the thought of a possible betrayal by him makes me nervous. For one he knows this building like the back of his hand, just like me. Suddenly my thoughts are broken because I see lights reflect off the wall and hear car doors being closed.

I hear voices in the back ground, sounds like six, maybe seven people. The voices are faint. Of course, I am five flights up. I quickly make my way to the closet window and peer out. All I can see is one vehicle I'm looking out the east side of the building try to get the best view possible but can't see how many more there are.

Then I hear the elevator start to come to life when I hear the sound of it starting up. I quickly realize either these guys are smarter than I gave them credit for or Mark did betray me. I will find that out very soon.

I run back to my hiding spot, trying to figure out quickly how and where exactly they are going to be and if they are just going to come out with guns blazing. Waiting for the sounds of the elevator door to open, I try to calm myself so I don't give away my location, but it's not as easy as you would think. The adrenaline is rushing through my body.

Then I hear the sounds of the elevator doors opening. Sounds I dreaded to hear. You can hear the footsteps rushing to the north and south sides of the fifth floor. My breathing is starting to pick up. I take a deep breath and hold it for a few seconds to try to slow it down. I have a small area where I can see out. I see no lights. I can't see anyone around. Of course, they don't want to give themselves up either so I sit and wait.

I no longer hear movement. Then I hear a familiar voice. No, it's not Edwards, but no other than the man I knew as one of my best friends, Mark.

He yells, "Mieser, you can come out now."

I knew it deep inside. It rips my heart out and infuriates me at the same time. I don't reply, but I do step out into the complete darkness. I do have a flashlight but I choose not to turn it on so as not to give away where I am. That is a surefire way to a quick death sentence.

Then I hear his voice again.

"Just give us what you have and we will leave you alone! I don't want to hurt you, Joe."

This statement makes me yell out, "Then why are you here and why did you betray our friendship?"

He chuckles and says, "You did that by sticking your nose where it didn't belong. Now give us what we want and we let you live."

"I'm not that stupid, Mark. You won't let me live even if I did give you what you wanted."

As I move around slowly toward the backside of the building toward the east side, not knowing where exactly the other men are, you could hear a pin drop in the building and there was no movement from the other guys at all so knowing where their location was going to be impossible.

I pull one of my guns out of the holster, then I hear Mark yell out, "You're right, we won't let you live. You see, Joe, you are very smart, but your downfall is that you just can't leave things well enough alone. I told you that night just to leave it alone, but you wouldn't listen. Too bad you couldn't realize it. It would have been in your best interest to have done what I said. But now you got yourself in a spot that you can't get out of."

"No, you should have never been involved with these people and you wouldn't be in the spot your going to be in. You see, Mark, I may not make it out of here alive, but I have things put in place that will put all of you in prison for the rest of your life, whether you kill me or I make it out of here alive."

I bought myself enough time to get to the east side spot where I have left some rope and where I can jump out of the window, but I need to be able to tie it to something strong enough to hold my weight. I search around in the dark and find a bar attached to the side of the wall. I quickly tie the rope to it. I just have to pray it's strong enough to hold if I need to jump out of it.

I move away from there because I'm a sitting duck if anyone turns on a light and head back the direction I was at. Then I hear, "Hit the lights." I stand up and run behind a pillar. There I have cover from any gunfire. The lights came on. I'm not talking the plant lights either, they would be stupid to do that 'cause people would then know something was going on and they would give themselves away. Work lights that construction workers used from all over it seemed lit up the room.

"Now, Joe, I'm giving you one more chance to give us those files."

"Not a chance," I yell back.

"Why don't you step out here and face me?"

"Tell your men to come out where I can see them, then maybe I will."

I hear Mark yell to his guys to come out where I can see them. I said, "No, I want them to be over by you!"

"Fine. Then you give us those files and you may just live to see another day."

I can now see all the men and Mark. I put my gun away and step out. I think to myself, Are you crazy putting your weapon away with a group of men fully armed wanting to kill you? Filled with rage by the fact that my best friend would betray me they way he did has taken all my fear away. I just want to wring his neck. Once out in the light, I stare right into Mark's eyes and I can guarantee if looks could kill he would have been dead the second I laid my eyes upon him. I clench my fist so tight I could feel my nails digging into my skin. Then I relax my hands and stare at Mark.

"Now give me the files," Mark says.

I chuckle at him and say, "Do you honestly think I'm just going to hand them over to you?"

Mark gets a sly smirk on his face as he starts gazing down at the floor. "You better." At that moment I realize it's going down.

I still have the backpack on my shoulders. I reach my hand slowly up to one of the shoulder straps of the backpack and act like I'm getting ready to pull it off. Instead, halfway up, I reach for the Beretta on my right side. With a rapid motion I have it out and a shot rings out, striking one of the thugs in the upper thigh. I quickly retreat behind the pillar. The lights go out again. I can hear rapid footsteps surround me once more. I hear rapid fire from their guns, and bullets ricochet off the pillar. I feel chunks of concrete strike me in the face as the bullets hit right next to me. I know I'm only going to have a few seconds from when they stop shooting to reload to get to a better place to protect myself. They empty their guns and I still have a full clip because I was only able to get one shot off.

It's now or never! I take a leap and tuck and roll. As I roll back up to my feet, I turn to my left. I hear the chambers of their gun click. They have reloaded. I point my gun in their direction and squeeze the trigger, running as fast as I can trying to dodge the onslaught of bullets whizzing past me. I dive into a small corner trying to gather myself. I feel something running down my arm. Not feeling any pain, I reach and feel my arm. I feel the blood streaming down. I've been hit, but the adrenaline is pumping through my body so I don't feel anything.

The shots keep coming and I can't stay here for too long, it's a death trap. I return fire, both guns blazing, trying to hit whatever moves. I jump to my feet and start running to where my rope is, but I'm blocked by the rapid gunfire aimed at me. I turn to run back to where I was, but by now I'm surrounded. There is no return and no escape. Just a square death trap that provides a little cover from the gunfire. I have to be able to get rid of a couple of these guys in order to get to my escape. I take a deep breath and slowly peak around the corner to see if I can see anyone. One shot comes whizzing by my head, missing by inches. Then I hear someone yell to hold fire.

"Joe, are you ready to give up those files yet?"

I step out of the shadows of the column, pull the backpack off my shoulders, and say, "This is what you want?" I can now see some faint figures in the background. I throw the pack to the right of me. When I see someone take off toward the pack, I shot him in the chest I don't hear anymore movement. One down, but I can't get the pack back.

"Just give it up!" Mark yells, "You're going to die."

"Not if I can kill you first," I yell in return.

Shots are fired. This time it sounds like a machine gun instead of just a pistol. I have to make a choice. There is going to be no way of taking these guys down, there is just too many of them. So it's either make a run for it or just sit here and die. Either way it's not going to play in my favor. I have made my decision, I'm running for it.

I take one big breath and take off. It feels like this is playing in slow motion. I can hear the chamber of the gun as it lets loose. Bullets fill the air. I'm running as fast as I can toward where I had placed the rope. I can hear the bullets as they pass by me and then I feel a pain in my leg then in my back. I drop to the floor. I can't just lay here and die this way. I get back to my feet and the bullets just keep coming. I finally get to the rope. I throw it out the window and get ready to jump, but I get hit again and I collapse immediately, hanging half over the window's edge and half inside the building's floor. I can't move, my breathing is slowing down, and I can hear the voices in the background along with footsteps coming behind me in rapid succession. I hear that familiar voice ordering the men to find me and make sure I was dead. That voice was of the man I knew as my best friend. I'm able to see below me a trash bin full of old trash praying that they aren't smart enough to shot me but to throw me off the edge I hear the footsteps right behind me and a man yells, "I got him."

Mark says to the man, "Don't do anything, let me do it."

Mark walks over to me looks down at me. "It's time for you to die." He grabs me and shoves me out the window, thinking I would just hit the ground instead of there being a trash can to break my fall.

They now think I'm dead. I land hard into the bin but don't feel a thing. I can't yell for help and I can't climb out of the trash can. But I can hear every little noise. I hear sirens in the background. Are they coming here? All I can do is hope, but I'm fading fast. My heart rate is dropping and my breath is even shallower than before. I hear the car doors slam shut and tires squealing in the distance. I can no longer keep my eyes open and my life starts to pass before my eyes.

I see everything, from the time I was a kid to when I became an adult all the memories of every moment I treasured. Times of my mom's homemade apple pies, her laughter, her soft touch when I would get hurt, and her stern voice when I did something wrong. My dad's quiet but tough demeanor he was a soft spoken and loving man but he was tough. All these memories flashed before my eyes. The memories of the childhood I shared with Mark. We played all the time with each other as we grew up. I could see all the football games and athletic events I went to with him all the way through our college years. We were best friends His smile and laughter and the good times we did share will always be some of my most treasured moments. The thoughts of the woman I loved from afar, Annie. Her smile could light up a room! Her eyes, I could get lost in them forever. She had a soft gentle voice and I know now that I should've never been such a coward and asked her out, but it's a little too late for that now. Snapped suddenly back into reality, I could feel my last deep breath of fresh air leave my body!

www.ingramcontent.com/pod-product-compliance
Lightning Source LLC
LaVergne TN
LVHW021739060526
838200LV00052B/3361